This Is How We Became a Family

AN ADOPTION STORY

Published by
M A G I N A T I O N   P R E S S
An Educational Publishing Foundation Book
American Psychological Association
750 First Street, NE
Washington, DC 20002

For more information about our books, including a complete catalog, please write to us,
call 1-800-374-2721, or visit our website at www.maginationpress.com

The text type is Garamond and Stuyvesant
Printed in Hong Kong
Editor: Darcie Conner Johnston
Art Director: Susan K. White

LIBRARY OF CONGRESS CATALOGING-IN-PUBLICATION DATA
Willis, Gordon Wayne, 1956-
This is how we became a family : an adoption story / written and illustrated by Wayne Willis.
p.   cm.
Summary: A childless husband and wife who want a baby adopt the child
of a young woman who cannot keep it.
ISBN 1-55798-666-5 (hardcover).   ISBN 1-55798-700-9 (paperback)
[1. Adoption—Fiction.] I. Title.
PZ7.W68312 Th 2000
[E]—dc21   99-055164

10 9 8 7 6 5 4 3 2 1

This Is How We Became a Family

AN ADOPTION STORY

written and illustrated by
WAYNE WILLIS

MAGINATION PRESS • WASHINGTON, DC

Part One: The Couple

O nce upon a time
there was a young couple
who had many of the good things in life.

They had a comfortable little home with a colorful little yard,

a reliable little car,

two good jobs,

several very good friends,

one playful cat,

and a marriage filled with love and affection.

And yet they were very sad
because they had no children.

After years and years
of trying and trying,
still they could not have a baby,
and finally the doctor told them
that they never would.

Then they were even more sad,
and they cried and cried
and cried.

Part Two: The Girl

Once upon a time, far, far away,
there was a young woman who could have a baby,
who, in fact, was already "expecting."

But she, too, was very sad.
"I'm too young to be a mother!" she cried,
and what she said was true.

She was hardly more than a girl herself.

She didn't have a home for a child.

She didn't have a job
to earn money to buy food
and warm clothing for a baby.

She didn't have a car
to drive to the store or to the park
or to the doctor.

She didn't even have a husband
to help her love and care for a baby.
"What am I going to do?" she cried.

She felt alone and confused
and was so sad she didn't know what to do.
And she cried and cried and cried.

Part Three: The Adoption

Once upon a time there was a place
where people helped solve the problems of other people
like the childless couple and the expectant girl.

The helpful people made phone call after phone call after phone call,

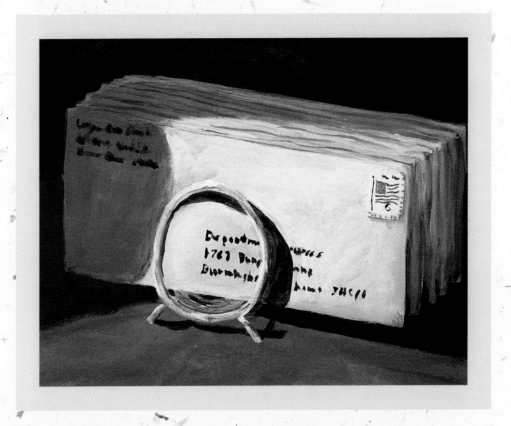

wrote letter after letter after letter,

filled out form after form after form,

and finally made it possible
for the childless couple,
who wanted a baby,
to adopt the baby,
who was born to the girl,
who was far too young to be a mother.

On the appointed day,
the girl presented the newborn child
to the childless couple,
and everyone cried some more.

The couple cried with happiness beyond words.
The girl cried with sadness, relief, and hope for the baby.
And the baby cried because that's what newborn babies do best.

Part Four: The Happy Ending

Soon the girl went back to her own youthful life,
the way it used to be.

She was not much older
but was now much, much wiser.

And the couple took their new baby
to their comfortable little home in their reliable little car
and began together a new life.
And from then on, the yard seemed even more colorful,
and the cat seemed even more playful,
and every day was filled with more joy than they had ever known.

Then the childless couple was childless no more,
and the expectant girl was expecting no more,
and the newborn baby was loved and adored.

And they all lived
as happily ever after
as "ever after"
ever really is.

For Suzannah

and Allison and Stephen
and Joy and John and James and Brandon
and Tyler and Tory and Jeremy and Brittainy
and Bill and Betsy and Bill and Nancy and Mike and Jill
and Leslie and Sarah and Lilee and Danna and Donna and Bill
and Emma Li and Martha and Catherine and Rebecca and Lon
and Samina and Brian and Molly and Nathan and Amy
and every other child who was ever the answer to someone's hopes, dreams, or prayers